# DODOS DON'T FLY

## MARK SIPPINGS

A NOTE ON THE AUTHOR

Mark Sippings was born in Walthamstow in 1959. He now lives in Essex. He has two daughters and a puppy called Millie Buttons.

www.marksippings.com

Cover & other illustrations: John Hepburn
www.jhepburn.co.uk

Book design & layout: John Hepburn

To the dreamers and imagineers

Mojo was a dodo but his real name was Colin because dodos weren't allowed to have unusual names. I'll tell you more about that later.

He lived on Dodo Island with his mum and dad, and his twin girls, Jane and Sarah.

It was a small island.

It was warm and cosy.

The sun shone, the sand was golden yellow, and the sea the deepest blue.

There was plenty of food and lots of ice-cold, crystal-clear water to drink.

Everyone was polite to each other and there was rarely a quarrel.

Everything should have been great but Colin was fed up.

Dodo Island was boring.

There were so many rules:

**Rule 1:** Dodos don't fly
**Rule 2:** No jumping
**Rule 3:** No climbing the mountain
**Rule 4:** No coloured feathers
**Rule 5:** No Rule 5
**Rule 7:** No going into the forest
**Rule 8:** Always – and that means ALWAYS – look down
**Rule 9:** No running
**Rule 10:** No unusual names
**Rule 11:** Absolutely no flying
**Rule 12:** No paddling

There were actually 127 rules, and these were always being added to. In fact, two more had been written in the time it's taken you to read this story.

At Dodo Nursery School, the children had to learn the rules like we have to learn our times tables: they repeated them over and over.

Very, very boring.

You might have noticed that there are two rules about flying in that list. In fact there are twenty-seven more on the subject. That's because dodos believe it is the most important rule of all.

You might also have noticed that there is no Rule 6. That's because many years ago there was a BIG argument on Dodo Island. An elder dodo, who was a bit of a clever clogs (you probably know the sort of dodo I mean), said that if there was no Rule 5 then Rule 6 became Rule 5 and it shouldn't be there either.

Half the dodos thought this was amazing, true and very, very clever, and wanted to be his best friend. The other half thought it was rather silly. It was the most excitement seen on Dodo Island EVER.

Some of the older birds fainted. Several younger ones from opposing sides glared at each other, breaking Rule 8.

Eventually, all the dodos sat in a big circle to discuss the rules, and despite one or two flying feathers, they agreed to rub out Rule 6 completely.

Everyone became friends again.

At school, young dodos soon learned not to ask why there was no Rule 5 and where Rule 6 had gone, because the teachers would become cross and say, 'Because. That's why.' However, I have a funny feeling they didn't know themselves. What do you think?

But all that was a very long time ago, and now the island was just boring. Well, perhaps that's not quite the right word. It was INCREDIBLY BOOOOOORING.

The dodos slept most of the day. The rest of the time they walked around searching for grubs. Sometimes – because they were not allowed to look up (Rule 8) – they would bump into each other. That would cause a flurry of feathers, a few apologies and, more often than not, tuts and beak-shaking from neighbours who'd say things like 'I would never have done that!' and 'Why can't people be more careful?'

But nothing much else happened.

You can see why Colin was fed up and bored.

And because he was fed up and bored, he was always asking questions.

'Why can't we paddle? It's so much fun and keeps me cool in the summer.'

'Why can't we look up?'

'Why can't we run about?'

Why? Why? Why? I expect you ask loads of questions, and perhaps sometimes your mum, dad or carer gets fed up and – just like the dodo teachers – says, 'Because. That's why.'

And that's what Colin's dad said to him.

Then one day, Colin said, 'Why can't we go into the forest, Dad?'

His dad sighed. He was a little sad that he didn't have the answers to most of Colin's questions. However, he knew the answer to this one. 'Because we are chickens, Colin.'

Which didn't make any sense at all. They were dodos, weren't they? Colin shook his head.

His dad continued. 'We peck around the farmhouse and most of us are happy with our lot. Still, some chickens want to go into the woods where the tastiest grubs are. But in the woods there is danger. I think you're one of those chickens, Colin, and that's why we need to have rules.'

Colin thanked his dad, but he was confused. Maybe Dad had spent a bit too long in the sun that day. Colin decided not to ask so many questions.

Remember Colin's two children, the twins Jane and Sarah? Well, he liked their names, but there were lots of dodos called Jane and Sarah. He'd really wanted to call them something unusual but Rule 10 made that impossible.

Most dodos thought the sensible-name rule was because of a sweet little dodo named Flower. Every time her parents had called her in for tea, all the other dodos would race over, hoping to see a new bloom (dodos like flowers). And when there wasn't one, they'd become cross.

So on the twins' naming day, instead of calling them Scarlet and Snowdrop, which is what Colin had wanted to do, he'd told the elders their names were

Jane and Sarah.

I suppose this is hardly surprising – Colin hadn't even told his own parents he'd prefer to be called Mojo.

To make matters worse, one day he'd been paddling in the beautiful blue sea (breaking Rule 12) when two strange objects floated by. They were square and about seven inches wide and long, but very thin. These were records, though what they're doing in a story that's at least a hundred years old, I don't know. The thing is, stories are magic, aren't they? And that means ANY-THING can happen.

The covers were soaking wet and rather faded, but

5

Colin could just make out the words on them: 'Hi Ho Silver Lining' and 'A Whiter Shade of Pale'. From that moment on, he knew his girls' real names would always be Scarlet Hi Ho Silver Lining and Snowdrop Whiter Shade of Pale.

The girls had pretended to be shocked and frightened when they first heard their real names but secretly they'd been rather pleased and would giggle and whisper the words when they snuggled up at bed time.

What sort of name do you have? Is it sensible or unusual? Would you change it if you could?

Dodos always slept standing up – Rule 83. Today, Colin was tired and his legs ached. He had been wandering around for hours under the blazing sun, searching for bugs. He'd found barely any and looked up from the sand. (I know, he broke another rule!)

In the distance, at the far end of the beach, stood the forest. It looked so cool and welcoming. A tiny idea began to form in his head. It grew and grew until he could think of nothing else. What if he were to creep over to it? He could lie down and no one would know. He might even find a few extra-tasty grubs. What harm could come from that?

Without another thought, he inched closer and closer to the trees, all the while pretending to look for food. As you can imagine, this took a while, and by the time he'd reached the forest he was even more tired. He glanced up, turned in a circle three times to make sure no one was watching, and leapt into the forest with a flutter (breaking Rule 8 and Rule 2).

It was a different world.

The trees sheltered the ground from the sun and it was so much cooler. But what made Colin's heart gal-

lop in his chest were the colours. Oh, the colours! They were breathtaking – bright reds and greens and golds.

Then again, it might have been the funny noises that made Colin's heart beat harder because they were a bit scary and Colin wasn't the bravest of birds. In fact, at that moment, he thought about breaking Rule 2 again and jumping straight back out. However, he took several deeps breaths, gave himself a shake, and continued walking.

Despite the caterwauling and the whooping, the rustling and the hooting, Colin started to relax and enjoy all the new smells and exciting colourful flowers. It was like being on holiday.

He came to a beautiful silver-blue lake that sparkled despite the lateness of the afternoon. Colin was very tired so he lay down and listened to the gentle rustle of leaves blowing in the breeze. The heather felt soft under his wings and the weight lifting from his legs was luxurious. It was as if they wanted to float into the sky all by themselves. The joy! He hadn't done this since he was little.

Colin closed his eyes and let his mind wander to the place of dreams … he was walking in the woods with his mum and dad. Scarlet and Snowdrop were by his side, sniffing the flowers and paddling in the blue lake. It was a wonderful, happy sleep.

* * *

Colin began to wake up.
If dodos had been able to smile, Colin would have.
Then he opened his eyes …
YIKES, IT WAS DARK!
How had he slept for so long? He felt very frightened.
He rubbed his eyes and looked upwards.
For the first time in his life he saw stars – millions of tiny silver pinpricks against the black night. His beak fell open at the spectacle. Never had he seen anything so beautiful. He stood and reached with his little wings, wanting to touch the shimmering lights, but they were too high.

Colin looked around, just to make sure no one was watching. The coast was clear.

He took a big hop and stretched his wings.

Nothing happened.

He used both legs to bounce off the ground, but still the glimmering stars remained out of reach.

Colin sighed. He knew he was breaking the rules. He shouldn't be in the woods, shouldn't be sleeping on his back, shouldn't be jumping, and shouldn't be looking up at the sky, but it was all too late now. He wanted to touch those stars so much his heart hurt.

He searched for something to stand on and jump from. Perhaps then he would be high enough.

And then he saw it, looming high above the trees. The mountain.

If he climbed to the top, surely he'd be among the silver sparkles. *I must go there before the other birds wake up*, he thought, and set off at a run (breaking Rule 9).

He reached the mountain and looked up – he'd broken that rule so often now that it didn't even seem like a rule anymore. It was much higher than he had imagined, ENORMOUS, in fact. How would he ever climb that? He shook his head, took a deep breath and began to hike up the steep slope.

Colin's claws slipped on the loose soil, and he tumbled and slid this way and that. He hopped over stones and pulled on weeds with his beak, hoisting himself along. For every step forward, he seemed to take two back, but he didn't give up.

After what felt like hours (but was probably only ten minutes), Colin had reached the summit. It was like being in outer space.

He stretched his wings, eager to grab a star or two, but try as he might he still couldn't reach them.

Colin felt sad. And hot and bothered. And out of breath. All that hard work for nothing.

He closed his eyes, leant forward and rested his wings. The cool breeze ruffled his feathers and after a while he began to feel a little better. He straightened, opened his eyes and looked down (just like Rule 8 said he should).

And gasped.

Below was the bottom of the mountain (okay, it was really a hill, but don't tell Colin that). He'd never been that high before. His head began to swim and patches of colour flashed in front of his eyes. He tottered and

teetered and teetered and tottered …

And then there was no mountain.

Colin began to fall.

He somersaulted once, twice, three times, and opened his wings to protect his head from the incoming ground …

And then he soared.

What on earth …?

He narrowed his eyes and peeped down.

He was high, REALLY high.

The dizziness came again, but Colin plucked up all his courage and looked. Far far below was the dark forest. It stretched over most of Dodo Island. All the other dodos were tiny little black dots asleep on the sand. Somewhere snug and safe in his nest were Scarlet and Snowdrop.

Emotion overwhelmed him – excitement, fear, but happiness too. Perhaps you've felt those things when you're about to get onto a scary ride. Colin's heart thundered so hard he was sure everyone would hear it.

But he didn't want to stop.

And wished more than anything that he could shout out his secret and share it with the whole world.

DODOS DO FLY!

He learned some other things, too, such as how important it was to keep flapping. He'd failed to do so and plummeted to the earth, missing the trees by millimetres. But then he'd fluttered furiously, feathers everywhere, and taken high into the air once more.

As the night went on, Colin got better at flying – just like when you first learn to ride a bike. To begin with you fall off all the time, but with practice you can do it.

Colin returned to his nest just as the island was waking up. Scarlet and Snowdrop jumped up and down with excitement and wanted to play Follow The Ant, their favourite game. They took hold of Colin's wings and pulled him towards their best ant's nest. But Colin was tired and said he had a tummy ache and needed to go back to bed.

* * *

The day dragged. Colin thought about nothing but flying, and when the twins spoke to him he barely heard them.

That night, he crept out of his nest, sneaked into the forest and climbed the mountain again.

He flew around and around, then far out to sea. He dived through the clouds, and down to the water, skimming it with his wings. He still couldn't reach the stars but it was as close to them as he'd ever been.

This happened every day for a week. Nothing else mattered – just his secret world. His favourite time was just before dawn. He would glide over the island on warm currents of air and watch the sun rise over the sea.

How could something so wonderful be wrong?

One morning, the elders called everyone together. They looked worried and said they had spotted a strange bird flying over Dodo Island. It was black and round with small wings and stubby feet. It looked like a dodo, which was silly because dodos didn't fly. They urged everyone to be careful – it might be one of the scary birds that stole dodo eggs.

Colin shuffled back into the crowd. His cheeks felt

very hot. And today, he paid particular attention to Rule 8 about always looking down.

Scarlett and Snowdrop looked fearfully at each other and then at their dad.

Colin made up his mind: NO MORE FLYING.

* * *

For a few days, things were as they had always been. Scarlet and Snowdrop seemed delighted when Colin began a game of Follow The Ant that led them on a winding tour of Dodo Island.

But each night, Colin glanced up at the stars and longed to fly again, even though he knew it was wrong. Flying was like chocolate, ice cream, birthdays and holidays all rolled into one. Not that Colin knew what those were, but perhaps you do.

After several sleepless nights, he could resist no longer. He waited until night fell, then crept out of bed and headed for the forest.

It began to rain but that didn't stop Colin. He soared among the clouds and dived towards the earth, pulling up at the last second. His heart raced.

Dawn broke and sunlight touched the earth and warmed his feathers. He hurried to the edge of the forest.

The twins stood on the sand at the treeline, blocking his way.

'Dad, what are you doing?'

'Nothing,' Colin said, feeling the heat rise in his cheeks once more.

'We saw you.'

'I wasn't doing anything. Come on. Let's go home and play Follow The Ant.'

'You were flying. That's not allowed.'

Colin laughed. 'No, no. Don't be silly. I wouldn't do that.'

'Dad we saw you. Why were you doing such a bad thing?'

There was sadness in their eyes and Colin felt terrible, worse than ever before. He'd told fibs to the most precious people in his life.

Scarlet and Snowdrop turned and walked away from him.

Colin hopped up behind and put a wing around each of their shoulders, but they shrugged him off and continued waddling.

'I'm so sorry,' he called out. 'I saw the stars and wanted to be with them.'

The twins turned.

'Promise you won't do it again, Dad. Please.'

Colin sighed, wishing with all his heart that he could reassure them, but he would never fib to them again.

'I can't,' he said.

Scarlet and Snowdrop hurried back to the nest without another word.

Colin let them go ahead. By the time he reached home, the twins were talking to his parents.

His dad looked at him aghast. 'Colin, what have you done?'

'I'm sorry, Dad, but I've discovered something wonderful. Why is it so wrong?'

'Because, that's why. You must stop flying.'

'I can't,' said Colin sadly.

'Then you must live somewhere else. If the elders find out you've been flying, we'll all have to leave Dodo Island, and that's not fair on the girls.'

His parents hugged the twins. Colin had never felt so sad.

He moved to the other side of the island and over the next few weeks he flew faster, higher and further than any dodo in history. He was no longer bored, no longer stifled by the rules.

And yet an emptiness tugged at his heart, as if he'd lost something special.

Colin missed his family.

Every night, he crept back to his old home and watched the twins sleeping. It didn't take away the empty feeling but at least he knew they were both safe.

He visited exotic islands and took a special treasure from each one. During his nocturnal visits home, he'd deposit the gifts in his old nest to remind his family that he still thought of them and cared.

Months passed by and Colin often wondered if flying was worth all the trouble it had caused. If he could only put the clock back to when he'd been happy with his old life.

But then he would open his wings and rocket towards the stars, and he knew that could never be. He would be alone for the rest of his days.

Then one day, Colin was out walking and something caught his eye in the grass – it glinted in the sunlight and he waddled over. There on the ground were four tiny silver stars – a single word on each:

*we love you always.*

He blinked back tears, picked up the stars and pressed them to his heart.

There was no time to lose. He rushed back to his old nest.

* * *

Scarlet, Snowdrop and his parents were waiting. Colin crashed into them, wrapped his wings around his family and kissed them.

'I love you so much,' he said.

The twins spoke in unison. 'We thought you liked flying more than us.'

Colin stood back and shook his head. 'Of course not! I'm so sorry I didn't explain things properly. Nothing is as important as you. I've seen and found a thousand fabulous treasures on my travels, but you are the most precious of all. There is no greater treasure.'

They cuddled again for what seemed like hours,

even when the other dodos tutted and huffed and said things like 'What is the world coming to?' and 'That kind of thing wouldn't have happened in my day.'

From that moment on, Colin and his family lived happily ever after. He kept his nest on the other side of the island but visited the twins every day, and played Follow The Ant and helped with their homework.

Sometimes Scarlet and Snowdrop worried when their dad left to go flying. What if he didn't come home? What if he began to love flying more than them? But it never happened. He always returned, ready with a big hug and a reminder that nothing was more precious than them.

* * *

The twins grew older and often sneaked out of bed and looked to the sky. Colin waved to them from on high as he weaved in and out of the stars.

Then one cold winter's day, three huge black shapes with billowing white sails appeared on the horizon. They approached the island and stopped near the shore.

Several large, two-legged creatures walked up the sandy beach, carrying spiderwebs tied to short branches. The elder dodos went to meet the strangers.

The strangers scooped up the elders and put them into brown sacks. The other dodos squawked in alarm and waddled up and down the beach. They made sure not to run or fly – that would have broken Rules 1, 9 and 11.

The poor dodos got nowhere fast, and soon all of them had been captured.

Can you guess who the creatures were and what they were holding?

Ask your mum and dad about dodos. They'll tell you there are none left. None at all in the whole wide world …

But … shh, this a secret! Don't tell anyone but I met one of the seamen who was on the island and he told me a story. While he was chasing the birds and popping them into his sack, he saw five dark shapes fly into the sky towards the stars. They looked a lot like dodos but he decided he must be seeing things because …

Dodos don't fly.

Do they?